Dino-mite!

The door to Mrs. Beak's room stopped him for a moment. It wasn't closed. It just wasn't there. He turned his head and saw it halfway down the hall, the glass in the top half completely blown away.

"Richie," he said softly.

"In here," said Richie, his voice excited.

Stepping carefully now to avoid the glass, David went into Mrs. Beak's room.

Desks were overturned and books were flung everywhere.

Richie was crouched in the corner. As David drew nearer, he saw Richie's dinotank. It was lying in a twisted, shattered heap on its side on the floor.

"Your dinotank!" said David. "Who's missing?" he asked, forgetting that he hadn't believed Richie, forgetting that he didn't believe it was possible for the dinosaurs to come back. . . .

Other Skylark Books you won't want to miss!

GRAVEYARD SCHOOL

5

Revenge of the Dinosaurs

Tom B. Stone

A SKYLARK BOOK

Toronto New York London Sydney Auckland

RL 3.6, 008–012

REVENGE OF THE DINOSAURS
A Skylark Book / March 1995

Skylark Books is a registered trademark of Bantam Books,
a division of Bantam Doubleday Dell Publishing Group, Inc.
Registered in U.S. Patent and Trademark Office and elsewhere.

Graveyard School™ is a registered trademark of
Bantam Doubleday Dell Publishing Group, Inc.

ISBN 0-553-48227-0

Published simultaneously in the United States and Canada

Bantam Books are published by Bantam Books, a division of
Bantam Doubleday Dell Publishing Group, Inc. Its trademark,
consisting of the words "Bantam Books" and the portrayal of a
rooster, is Registered in U.S. Patent and Trademark Office and in
other countries. Marca Registrada. Bantam Books, 1540
Broadway, New York,
New York 10036.

PRINTED IN THE UNITED STATES OF AMERICA

OPM   0 9 8 7 6 5 4 3 2 1

GRAVEYARD SCHOOL

5

Revenge of
the Dinosaurs

CHAPTER
1

The reptile grabbed her in his terrible teeth. His head was so big, his jaws so huge, that only her feet stuck out. They were ugly feet. They kicked. But she didn't make a sound.

Still holding his victim, the terrible lizard bent down, looking for more treats. The terrible claws on its forefeet twitched in anticipation as it leaned forward . . .

A bony hand clamped down on David Pike's shoulder.

He screamed.

The kids around him started to laugh as the terrible Mrs. Beak, the nastiest teacher in the whole school, claimed her latest victim.

"You *were* paying attention, weren't you, David?" she asked softly. She had the softest, meanest voice David had *ever* heard.

"Yes," said David. He swallowed hard. "I was, ah, thinking."

"And what do you think the answer is?" Mrs. Beak asked, her hand tightening on David's shoulder.

David's gaze went back to the lizard tank, where the class's pet lizard was finishing its lunch of live beetle. Even the beetle's legs had disappeared.

David had been imagining that the beetle was Mrs. Beak.

No such luck.

"Well? We're waiting. Enlighten us with the answer," said Mrs. Beak in her soft, mean voice.

"Uh, I don't know." *It's got to be the red flannel shirt,* he thought wildly. If he hadn't worn red, maybe Mrs. Beak wouldn't even have noticed him. Mrs. Beak seemed attracted to the color red. She wore it all the time. Like the red ribbon she had tied around her neck, as if her head had been whacked off and reattached.

Mrs. Beak's hand tightened even more. "You don't know? *You don't know?*" She let go of David's shoulder and lurched to the front of the room, her fists raised. David slumped down in his seat, rubbing his shoulder.

"For *this* I went to college? So you could ignore me? So you could not do your homework and not listen in class and then tell me *you don't know?*"

David didn't answer. It seemed the safest course of action.

He was wrong.

Mrs. Beak fastened her steely gaze on him. The rest of the kids in her sixth-grade class all seemed to move away from David somehow. Perfect Polly Hannah, who never got in trouble, stared down at her perfectly neat notebook as if she'd suddenly detected a smudge on it. Jaws Bennett, who lived to eat and would eat anything, suddenly stopped chewing his gum and swallowed it. Even David's best friend, Raul Perez, looked away.

"Perhaps a conversation with Dr. Morthouse would have a positive effect on your attention span in my class, David. What do you think?"

"No!" said David before he thought.

Mrs. Beak's small blue eyes, so close together that they looked as if they pinched her nose, brightened. "No? No? You don't think that talking to Dr. Morthouse would improve your behavior in my class, David? Well, I have to disagree, if you don't mind. You don't mind if I disagree, do you?"

Polly Hannah giggled.

Teacher's pet, thought David disgustedly. Someday Polly Hannah was going to get it, really get it.

But not today. Today, it seemed, was David's day.

Mrs. Beak smiled a saber-toothed smile in Polly's direction. Then she bent over her desk and scribbled out a pass to the office. After that, she wrote several sentences on a piece of paper, folded it up, and popped it into an envelope. She sealed the envelope.

"I'm sending Dr. Morthouse a little note, along with your pass to her office."

David stood up and walked to the desk where Mrs.

Beak stood, the note and the pass in her outstretched hand. He took the note, being careful not to touch the Beak's hand, and walked to the door, his back stiff, his eyes straight ahead.

"David?" said Mrs. Beak when he reached the door.

David turned. He met Mrs. Beak's eyes.

"See you later, David," said Mrs. Beak.

The halls of Graveyard School were empty. Not even Basement Bart, Mr. Bartholomew, the weird janitor from the dark side, was pushing his stringy mop down the hall.

For a moment, David contemplated not going to the office. He thought about ducking into the boys' bathroom, waiting a suitable amount of time, then going back to Mrs. Beak's room.

"Oh, yes," he'd say, giving her a big mean smile to match her own. "Dr. Morthouse and I had a little talk. She wanted me to tell you that *you're fired!*"

It was a nice thought. But it could never happen. And the pleasure of actually doing something like that wouldn't last long enough to overcome the extreme trouble he would find himself in with his parents immediately afterward.

Besides, he had to bring the note back signed by Dr. Morthouse.

He hated Mrs. Beak.

He wasn't the only one. Mrs. Beak had been hated by sixth graders for several years now. It was particularly hard for David, though, because he actually liked science.

But that didn't matter to Mrs. Beak. David suspected that, in reality, Mrs. Beak hated science. She often made nasty speeches about the environment and made fun of environmentalists. "So what if a few oil tankers kill a few dumb animals? We need oil!" she'd said more than once. She never recycled, throwing her soda cans into the garbage, wrapping her lunches in plastic.

She even smoked cigarettes. David had seen her, careening into the teachers' parking lot in her huge, gas-guzzling car, with smoke pouring from the tail-pipe—and smoke pouring out of her nose before she stubbed out her cigarette.

David looked up and realized he'd reached the principal's office. He squared his shoulders and walked in.

Mr. Kinderbane, the office manager, looked up. He raised one of his jutting, hairy eyebrows. "Yesss?"

"Uh, I, uh, need to see Dr. Morthouse?"

"Do you now?"

"Uh, yes. Mrs. Beak sent me. Here's a note."

"Ah." Mr. Kinderbane sounded pleased. He extended his hand and plucked the note from David's cold fingers.

"Sit there," he said, pointing to one of two uncomfortable orange chairs by the door. A more comfortable chair stood in the corner. David had never seen a student in that chair.

Why should I suffer? thought David. Ignoring Mr.

Kinderbane, he marched over to the comfortable chair and sat down.

He looked up. Mr. Kinderbane was frowning so ferociously that his two hairy eyebrows looked liked one.

Mr. Kinderbane folded his arms.

David folded his arms.

At last Mr. Kinderbane said, "Hmmmph!"

He turned and marched toward the principal's office, holding the note in the air like a victory flag.

I hate Mr. Kinderbane, too, thought David.

He didn't get to wait in the comfortable chair long. Mr. Kinderbane marched back out and announced, "Dr. Morthouse will see you. *Now.*"

"Gee, thanks," said David sarcastically. But he didn't say it loudly enough for Dr. Morthouse to hear him through her partially open office door.

At least, he hoped not.

When David came in, Dr. Morthouse was writing something on a piece of paper at her desk. She didn't look up. She didn't invite him to sit down. Her dark head remained bent over her work.

David cleared his throat.

Dr. Morthouse ignored him.

The silence in the room grew and grew. Although it was a cool day, David began to sweat. He knew Dr. Morthouse was trying to psych him out.

It was working.

In desperation, David turned slightly to peer through the slatted blinds at Dr. Morthouse's window. But the blinds were closed. It was a bright, sunny day, but the principal clearly didn't want any part of it.

David turned back to Dr. Morthouse's desk to find her watching him.

"According to Mrs. Beak, you have an attention problem, David," said Dr. Morthouse. "I can see her point."

"B-B-But . . . ," David sputtered.

"She says you're argumentative, too."

"I'm not!" cried David, stung by the injustice of it all. Adults. You couldn't live without them and you couldn't feed them to the lizards.

Ugh.

"You're a good student, David. Until this year, I haven't seen you in the office all that often . . ." Dr. Morthouse paused. She picked up a pair of half-glasses and put them on and examined the note from David's teacher again. Her expression as she read it made David uneasy. What else did the note say?

Dr. Morthouse glanced up. She was a frightening-looking person at the best of times. Now the lack of expression on her face made her truly terrifying.

David felt like an insect beneath a microscope.

But all the principal said was "Mrs. Beak . . . hmmm." Abruptly she scribbled something at the bottom of the note. She put it back in the envelope and stood up so suddenly that David involuntarily jumped back.

If Dr. Morthouse noticed, she didn't show it. She

handed the note to David and said, "Remember, you have a little brother at this school for whom you must set an example. Let's try to get back on track, shall we?"

David was so stunned, he only nodded. But that seemed to satisfy Dr. Morthouse. She sat back down.

David stood there, waiting to get in more trouble.

Dr. Morthouse started writing again.

David cleared his throat.

Dr. Morthouse looked up. She seemed surprised. "Is there something else I can help you with?" she asked.

"No—nothing!" said David. He turned and ran out the door of the principal's office before she could change her mind.

Mr. Kinderbane handed David a pass back to his class.

"Thanks!" said David. He gave Mr. Kinderbane a big smile, just to drive him crazy.

His smile was even bigger as he handed Mrs. Beak his note. *Take that,* he thought. *Dr. Morthouse didn't even give me detention, ha, ha, ha . . .*

Mrs. Beak turned the note over as if she couldn't believe her eyes.

Then she looked up. "Sit down."

David turned triumphantly to go to his seat. For the rest of the class, he was a model student. He watched Mrs. Beak like a hawk. He never looked at the lizard tank. He forced himself to concentrate on everything she said about vertebrates and invertebrates. He pretended that she wasn't making science, his favorite subject, the most boring thing in the world.

He hardly blinked, just like the lizard in the lizard tank.

He knew that Mrs. Beak was watching him, too.

The bell rang at last. David practically leaped from his seat. His eyes itched from paying attention so hard.

Mrs. Beak stopped him as he lunged for the classroom door. "David."

Reluctantly, David turned. Mrs. Beak was crooking a thin finger at him, beckoning him closer. He walked to her desk and stopped as far away as possible.

"I have to get to my next class," he said. "It's a really good class and I don't want to be late."

Two spots of color grew darker on Mrs. Beak's pale cheeks.

Student and teacher glared at each other for a long moment. Then Mrs. Beak said, "Fine. But report back to me after school. Dr. Morthouse may not see fit to do more than talk to you, but you're going to stay after school today."

David's mouth dropped open. Mrs. Beak smiled her thinnest, meanest smile.

"Enjoy your next class," she said.

CHAPTER

2

"This means war," said David.

Raul said, "Take it easy. It's just one day."

"Would you say that if it was you?"

"Nope," said Raul, grinning. He and David were standing at their lockers waiting for David's little brother, Richie, who was in the first grade. Richie was just coming down the hall now, his head bent over a book, reading as he walked.

Just like their father. Their father was a scientist, an astronomer. He was always doing research and flying all over the world to conferences. And he was always reading, too.

"Chill," said Raul. "I'll walk Dino-head home."

"Thanks," said David. Without looking up from his book, Richie walked toward the two boys. David put out his hand and stopped Richie by pressing his palm against Richie's forehead.

"What are the chances of Mrs. Beak getting eaten by a dinosaur, Dino-head?"

Richie looked up at last. Sure enough, the book he was reading was about dinosaurs. *Dinosaurs,* the title read. *More Than Terrible Lizards.*

"Dinosaurs are extinct," he said sadly. "They've been extinct for at least sixty-five million years."

"Then you're outta luck, David," Raul said, laughing.

"You sure about that?" David said. "That they're extinct? All of them?"

Looking seriously at his older brother, Richie said, "Yes." He added, "No one knows why. Some believe they were killed off by a giant volcano. Some scientists think an asteroid hit the earth. Some scientists think that out in space—"

"Little guys from Mars. That's what did it," David joked.

Richie opened his mouth to protest and explain. He had no sense of humor that David could see, especially when it came to dinosaurs. Quickly David cut in, before Richie could get started. "Have to stay late today," he said. "So go with Raul. Tell Dad I'll be home soon."

"Okay," said Richie.

"Good luck," said Raul. He and Richie headed off down the hall.

David started for Mrs. Beak's room. Of course he knew dinosaurs were extinct. He'd been a dinosaur freak himself once. Not as bad as Richie, of course. But he knew all about the theories of extinction.

He still thought it would be a great way for Mrs. Beak to go. Pushing open the door of her room, he walked in.

Mrs. Beak was ready for him. She pointed at the desk in front of her own. "You will write one thousand times, 'I will pay attention in Mrs. Beak's class,' " she said.

David gave Mrs. Beak a big smile.

Mrs. Beak glared and went back to her desk. "One thousand times," she repeated. She sat down and began to read a magazine.

Picking up his pen, David thought, *Maybe death by dinosaur is too good for her. . . .*

"Hello, I'm home! If anybody cares!" David staggered through the back door into the kitchen of the old house at the edge of Grove Hill where his family lived. He knew his mother was probably still at her office. But he'd decided to live dramatically anyway.

"I'm home and I'm injured. Seriously!" He dropped his pack on the kitchen floor and flung himself down on the old wooden floorboards. Gripping his right wrist in his left hand, he held both hands over his head. Writing that stupid sentence a thousand times really had done something funny to his hand.

Maybe he'd never be able to use it again.

Just then Mr. Pike wandered into the kitchen holding a book. He looked down at his older son with an expression of mild surprise on his face. "Is something wrong?"

David looked up at his father from the floor. The angle made his father's round stomach look even more rounded. It made his head look tiny and far away.

"Mrs. Beak," said David. "My science teacher. I had to stay after school."

"Extra credit?" asked Mr. Pike. "That's nice." He wandered out again.

Then a voice spoke in David's ear. "Are you dead?"

"No, I'm extinct," said David, rolling his eyes. He sat up. His little brother was squatting on the floor next to him. Richie was holding a brown box stamped all over with various warnings in bright red letters: THIS SIDE UP. HANDLE WITH CARE. FRAGILE. DO NOT EXPOSE TO HEAT OR COLD. DO NOT EXPOSE TO HIGH-INTENSITY LIGHT. "New dinosaurs, Lizard Lips?" David asked his brother.

Richie nodded, his eyes shining. "A new *Tyrannosaurus rex!*"

"That's nice," said David.

"William bit the head off my old one," said Richie, referring to the fat, cranky cat that shared the house with the Pikes. The cat had been at the house longer than the Pikes had. He'd been there when they'd moved in, sitting on the top step, and he'd never left.

William hated all small animals, alive or made of plastic. He could often be found, especially during

14

long, cold, boring winter days, staring hungrily at the dinosaur figures in Richie's dinosaur terrarium, the tip of his tail lashing.

"I remember. Tough luck," said David.

"Yes. But the place I got it from had another one. Only it cost more this time."

"Yeah," said David, getting up. His hand was less numb now. Maybe he could hold a soda.

Richie followed David to the refrigerator. "I'm about to introduce the *T. rex* to its new home," said Richie. "Want to see?"

"Sure." David poured out a soda, then followed Richie to his room.

Only it was more like a museum. The little dino-head had filled every available shelf with dinosaurs and dinosaur stuff. Posters and time lines hung on the walls, showing the different dinosaurs and the different prehistoric periods in which they'd lived. A dinosaur mobile floated from the ceiling. Stuffed dinosaurs spilled out of the chair in the corner. Dinosaurs decorated the sheets and pillowcases on Richie's bed.

It made David dizzy just to look into Richie's room. But of course it didn't bother Richie. Ignoring it all, he charged over to the enormous fish tank that stood on the old toy chest in the corner. One side of the tank was cracked. The owners of the local pet supply store, The Animals' House, had given it to Richie because it was broken.

The tank was Richie's prize possession. He had

landscaped it with rocks and dirt and a little blue saucer of water to make a pond. Small plants grew in the dirt. There was even a mountain with a cave in the bottom of it. The dinotank, Richie called it. All his favorite model dinosaurs lived there.

Richie set the box down by the terrarium. He reverently reached inside and parted the tissue paper. Carefully, gently, he took out a tiny figure.

"Here he is," said Richie. *"Tyrannosaurus rex."*

"Yeah, I know. Even I know what a tyrannosaurus is, Richie. I mean, everybody does."

"The biggest, meanest hunter that ever lived," Richie continued. "Its name means 'king of the ruling lizards.' Ten tons, up to six-inch teeth, nineteen feet tall, fifty feet long—"

"I hate to disappoint you, Fossil Face," interrupted David. "But the dinosaur you're holding should be called *Tiny-saurus rex.* It's only a few inches long. Have you checked that out?"

The faraway look left Richie's eyes. "Shhh!" he said. "He doesn't know that." He cradled the tiny plastic dinosaur protectively in his hand, then leaned over and set it in the dinotank in front of the cave.

"Sorry, didn't mean to hurt his little dinosaur feelings," said David.

Richie ignored him. "Hi," he crooned, peering down into the dinotank. "Welcome to your new home. I think you'll like it, Trex." He turned his head. "That's what I'm gonna call him, see? Trex. Get it? T-rex?"

"Got it," said David. He gave his little brother a thump on the shoulder. "Trex is a very nice dinosaur. He looks . . ."

David stopped and bent over. The tiny figure stood upright on its two thick hind legs in front of the cave. It had two small front feet, each of which had two curved, swordlike claws. The skin was mottled in different colors, not unlike the lizards in the lizard tank at school. The mouth was open and the teeth looked sharp and shiny.

And the eyes were cold and dark, just like Dr. Morthouse's.

The *Tyrannosaurus rex* might not be life-sized, but it looked lifelike. *Very* lifelike.

"Where'd you get this guy?" David asked.

"In the mail from Cosmic Dinosaurs," answered Richie, studying his new acquisition. "It's a dinosaur specialty company near where the first tyrannosaurus bones were found." When Richie talked about dinosaurs, he always sounded as if he were answering a question on a test.

David watched the tiny dinosaur for a minute longer. His brother had always treated his dinosaurs as if they were real. He pretended to feed them and talk to them, and more than once he'd insisted they were growing.

It had never bothered David before. He'd always thought it was kind of weirdly funny.

But for some reason, this dinosaur was giving him the creeps.

At last he tore his eyes away. Mrs. Beak had fried his brain. That was the only explanation.

"Welcome to the dinotank, big guy," he said to the dinosaur. "Later," he said to his brother.

Richie didn't answer. He was still glued to the scene inside the dinotank, like someone waiting for a movie to begin.

At the dinner table, David managed to duck his parents' questions about school by encouraging Richie to talk about his new dinosaur.

"He's very smart," Richie told everyone. "But he keeps looking at the triceratops. I think he's hungry. . . ."

"Don't let him get out," Mrs. Pike teased. "He might eat William!"

Naturally Richie didn't get it. He shook his head, his eyes round. "Oh, no," he said. "William's the one who bit the head off my *other T. rex*."

"What a cat-astrophe. Get it? A *catastrophe*," David said. His parents both laughed, and forgot about school.

Which still leaves the problem of Mrs. Beak, thought David as he lay in bed that night. His wrist was throbbing. Doing homework on top of writing a thousand stupid sentences hadn't helped. But he'd made sure he got his science homework done.

He was at war with Mrs. Beak. He wasn't going to give her the satisfaction of giving him bad grades.

Mrs. Beak. Ugh. But then, she wasn't the only weirdo at Graveyard School, after all. The school, which was really named Grove Hill Elementary School, or Grove School for short, was called Graveyard School by all the students not only because it stood out on the edge of town next to an old abandoned graveyard, but also because of the exceedingly weird things that happened there all the time.

Weird, sometimes horrible things. Things that had no logical explanation. Things that the adults, somehow, never seemed to notice.

But then, the people in charge of Graveyard School were pretty *Twilight Zone* themselves. Like Dr. Morthouse, whose voice sounded like frozen gravel in a can. She appeared to be able to hear through walls and see around corners. And everyone said she had a silver fang in her mouth.

Just as weird, but in a much less scary way, was Hannibal Lucre, the assistant principal. He was a wobbly plump man who almost always wore brown suits and blindingly bright bow ties. The worst thing about him was that he always combed forward a long strand of hair in a vain attempt to hide his bald spot. He was fond of telling all the students, "The principal is your pal."

But then there was Basement Bart. Some said he lived in the heating system that ran through the school . . . that he'd made a maze of tunnels connecting the school to the graves on the hill above the school . . . that . . .

David turned over and pulled the blanket up. He yawned. He'd never had a problem with ole Bart. His problem was with Mrs. Beak. Why was Mrs. Beak a teacher when she so clearly hated students? Why had they ever hired her to teach at Graveyard School?

Why did she hate him, David, worst of all her students? Could she really still hold it against him that he'd corrected her in class when she made that stupid mistake about the rotation of the earth around the sun and some of the kids had laughed?

He wondered if he should talk to his mother and father about Mrs. Beak.

Nah.

He could handle it himself. He'd think of something.

Maybe he'd figure out some way to shrink her down to beetle size and feed her to the class lizard for real. Imagining that, he fell asleep with a smile on his face.

"David."

The monster turned. It was a giant *Tyrannosaurus rex*. Blood dripped from its teeth.

Then David realized that the *T. rex* didn't have a normal *T. rex* head.

Instead, it was the head of Mrs. Beak.

"David," she said in her soft, mean voice, opening her mouth wide and then gnashing her bloody teeth . . .

"ARRRRRGh!" screamed David. *"No! No! Get away from me!"*

"AAaah!" a little voice shrieked in David's ear, and something hit David in the head.

It was a pillow.

"Hey!" gasped David, struggling to get free of the pillow, the blanket, and the nightmare.

He fell out of the bed and found himself face-to-toes with his brother's bare feet.

Quickly he sat up. Richie was standing by the bed in his striped pajamas, his hair sticking up all over the place. He was holding a flashlight in one hand and hopping from one foot to the other in excitement.

"Did you hit me with the pillow? What'dja do that for?" David complained.

"You scared me," said Richie, as if it were the simplest thing in the world. He kept hopping. "David . . ."

"You hit me with a pillow in the middle of the night again, you're gonna be more than just scared," David threatened. "What are you doing in my room?"

"It's my dinosaur," Richie said breathlessly, his voice going up to a squeak. "My new dinosaur, Trex. He's escaped!"

CHAPTER
3

"You woke me up for *that*?" David growled. "I don't believe it."

"Something woke me up," Richie went on. He looked like a demented gnome.

"Stand still," David commanded, grabbing the flashlight. The zigzagging of the beam of light was making him dizzy.

"So I got up and looked in my dinotank."

"Where else?" muttered David sarcastically.

Richie didn't notice. "And that's when I realized it: Trex wasn't there! He'd escaped."

"Richie, Trex couldn't have escaped. He's a plastic dinosaur. Even if dinosaurs weren't extinct, it would be very, *very* hard for a plastic anything to escape from anywhere."

"He's not plastic," said Richie. "Guaranteed."

"What are you talking about now?" David asked as Richie sat down on the bed.

"Cosmic Dinosaurs guarantees that they're not made of plastic! 'Only authentic materials!' " Richie quoted in an agitated voice.

David would have rolled his eyes, but it would have been wasted in the dark. "Yeah, right," he said. The kid was worked up, no doubt about it. "Look, Richie, I'll go back to your room and check the dinotank out for you, okay?"

"But . . ." Richie's voice went up again.

"Shhh!" David said, leading the way to the door with the flashlight. "Or you'll wake Mom and Dad."

Richie stopped talking.

When David reached his little brother's room, he pulled Richie inside. He pushed the door almost shut and turned on the light.

"See?" whispered Richie loudly. "See?" He rushed over to the dinotank and pointed down.

David looked where Richie was pointing. Sure enough, the screen top was off the dinotank. The dirt in front of the miniature cave where Trex had been standing was all clawed up. The miniature trees had been uprooted. The grass had been trampled.

Remembering the tiny, wicked pair of claws on the stubby front feet of the toy tyrannosaurus, David felt a sudden chill. Was it possible? Had Trex actually come to life? Had he broken out of his new home?

It wasn't possible. It couldn't happen. David swallowed hard.

24

Then he saw something else: a muddy paw-print on the side of the glass. He was suddenly very, very relieved.

"Richie, look." David pointed. "That's a cat's paw-print. Your dinosaur didn't escape. William kidnapped it!"

"William?" Richie leaned over to peer at the paw-print. His chocolate-brown eyes narrowed. He ran his hand through his hair in agitation, so that it stood up like the spiky armor on one of his dinosaurs. *"William!"*

"Shhh!" David warned.

"I'm gonna kill William," said Richie, ignoring David.

Suddenly, as if Richie's words had actually frightened him, William shot out from under Richie's bed.

"Stop him!" cried Richie.

David leaped for the door, but it was too late. William streaked through.

He was holding something in his mouth.

"Get him!" Richie shrieked.

"Shhhhhhh!" David said. But he ran after William, with his little brother right behind him.

William raced down the hall. He took the turn at the top of the stairs so sharply that the rug skidded out from under him. For a moment, he ran madly in place.

David lurched for the big cat.

But even though William was big and fat and old, he

was still a cat. He got a grip on the bunched-up rug just in time and leaped forward down the stairs.

Richie practically trampled David as he went by.

"Hey!" David said, forgetting his own warnings to be quiet. He scrambled up and rejoined the chase.

The three of them tumbled down the stairs and raced down the hall to the kitchen.

William reached the cat door well ahead of them, but, as always, it was going to take him a moment to squeeze his fat body through.

"Ha!" shouted Richie, grabbing the cat's tail.

"Mrrrrrow!" howled William in outrage.

"He's gonna kill you, Richie! Let him go!"

"No way! He's got my dinosaur. I'm not letting go till he gives Trex back." Richie gave a fierce backward pull on William's tail.

Somehow William got his back claws into action.

"Oowww!" cried Richie. He let go of William and fell backward.

William popped through the door like a cork out of a bottle and was gone. *"MEEEeeeoooo . . . ,"* they heard him yowl, triumphant, as he raced into the night.

"Are you okay?" asked David. He flicked on the kitchen light. Bright red scratches ran down both of Richie's arms.

Richie didn't bother to answer. He was already getting to his feet and opening the back door. "We've got to catch him," he panted. "We've got to!"

He flung open the door and stopped. At the edge

of the square of light spilling out from the kitchen, the *T. rex* lay on its side.

Richie squatted down anxiously. He picked the dinosaur up and held it in the palm of his hand. "He's okay!" he told David joyously. He held up his hand toward David. David bent forward to look.

Just then a blinding light filled the night.

Instinctively David jerked his hands up to cover his eyes. Richie did the same, dropping the dinosaur on the ground.

The light was so bright that David could see it even with his eyes closed. Brighter than lightning. Brighter than day. It was as if a giant camera had suddenly flashed. A humming sound filled the air and a whoosh of air swirled around them.

Then the light went out.

Slowly, cautiously, David lowered his hands. For a moment he couldn't see anything. Then his eyes gradually adjusted to the darkness and the now dim-seeming light coming from the kitchen.

"Wow," said David. "I wonder what that was."

"A flying saucer," said Richie instantly.

"We'll have to ask Dad if there was supposed to be a shooting star or something tonight . . . or maybe it was some kind of weird lightning," David went on, ignoring Richie.

Richie shrugged. He bent down. "Hey, look! When I dropped Trex, he landed on his feet! Isn't that neat?"

"Cool," said David absently, studying the sky. It was

a clear night, no moon. The stars all looked pretty normal.

Reaching down, Richie picked up the toy dinosaur again. "Owww!"

"Now what?" said David, looking down at his brother.

"He dug his claws into my hand. . . ." Richie raised the dinosaur on the palm of his hand to eye level. "Bad Trex," he said. "Bad boy."

"Hey, it's a fake dinosaur, remember?" said David. He'd just realized how late it was and how sleepy he felt.

"He did," Richie insisted. "See?" He lifted the dinosaur off his hand and turned his palm toward David. David could see what looked like red scratches.

"Good one, Dino-head. That's not from your toy dinosaur, that's from William. Now let's go in the house."

"It is from Trex!" Richie insisted. "Don't worry, Trex. I'll put you back in your cave and you'll be safe from that big old cat. . . . I'm sure glad William didn't bite his head off, aren't you, David? David?"

They had reached Richie's room. David opened the door and pointed. "Go to bed," he said.

"First I have to put Trex to bed," said Richie.

"Whatever," said David wearily. He suddenly felt like a weird adult-type person. What was his little brother doing to him? "Just turn off the light before you go to sleep."

"Okay," said Richie happily.

"G'night," David said, closing the door with a sigh of relief. As usual, Richie didn't even hear him. He was already bent over the dinotank, talking to his dinosaurs.

CHAPTER
4

"You didn't see any, like, shooting stars last night, did you?" David asked Raul as Raul came up the front steps of Graveyard School.

Raul thought for a moment, then shook his head slowly. Raul never rushed into anything. He was always very calm. *Maybe that's why he does so well in school,* David thought.

"I think I did," David went on, studying the crowd of students gathering on the stairs before school. The sixth graders were assembling at the top. Down below, on the very bottom of the steps, David could see his little brother's head among the crowd of first graders.

What a doofus Richie is, thought David. He yawned. Maybe it *had* been a shooting star. He didn't think so, but there didn't seem to be any other logical explanation.

Oh, well. It wasn't a big deal. The big deal was Mrs. Beak, whom he would have to face that afternoon.

"How did it go with the Beak?" asked Raul.

Polly Hannah, standing nearby with Stacey Carter and Maria Medina, overheard Raul's question. "David had to stay after school yesterday," she announced loudly, as she removed her blue velvet bow barrette and readjusted it in her neat blond hair. The blue bow matched Polly's blue tights and the flowers in her blue corduroy skirt.

"Did you have to stay long, David?" Polly went on with false sweetness.

David lost his patience. "Are you related to Mrs. Beak or something?" he blurted out. "'Cause you're just as disgusting."

Polly's face turned red. Her mouth dropped open.

Stacey started to laugh and quickly turned it into a cough. Maria laughed aloud and pretended to be pounding Stacey on the back.

Even Raul smiled. "Target!" he said.

Recovering her wits, Polly said, "Well, for your information, David Pike, I happen to like Mrs. Beak!"

Everyone around them froze.

Polly's face turned even redder. "Well, she's always wearing new clothes—and—and—she's not so bad," she stammered.

Stacey said, "Did some alien spaceship come down last night and suck your brain, Polly? Mrs. Beak's not bad—she's *awful.*"

"Infinitely awful," said Maria.

"The worst of the worst," said Raul.

"Shhhh," said David. He had spotted two familiar figures at the bottom of the stairs.

The students parted as Dr. Morthouse and Mrs. Beak came up to the front door of the school. The two adults were deep in conversation and hardly seemed to notice the kids pressing back away from them on either side.

They made quite a contrast. Dr. Morthouse wore her navy pinstriped suit, and her expressionless face was framed by her dark, chin-length hair and the same pointed silver earrings she wore almost every day. The low heels of her shoes struck each stone step with a solid thunk. Mrs. Beak's flat gray shoes slid softly up the stairs. She wore a short gray skirt with pearly stockings, and a short red jacket over a white blouse. Her earrings were little red flowers, and her hair was fluffy and yellow and soft-looking.

Mrs. Beak looked as if she'd stepped out of a magazine. Dr. Morthouse looked as if she'd stepped out of a prison.

Mrs. Beak turned her head and met David's eyes. She stared at him for a long moment.

Dr. Morthouse said something and Mrs. Beak turned back toward the principal as the two of them walked into the school.

"Wow," said Raul softly. "Did you see that look she gave you?"

"I saw," said David. "I saw."

•   •   •

Several hours later, David was sitting rigidly upright in Mrs. Beak's science class. The strain of paying attention was making him sleepy. But he didn't dare just pretend he was paying attention.

He and Mrs. Beak were watching each other like hawks.

At least he was prepared this time when she hit him with a question.

"And what caused the extinction of the dinosaurs? Any theories, anybody?" The class was silent. It was a question on material they hadn't read yet.

Mrs. Beak waited a moment longer. Then she swooped down for the attack. "David?"

Raul raised his hand bravely, trying to help David out. "Mrs. Beak, we haven't read that part of the book yet!" he called out, without even waiting.

The look Mrs. Beak gave Raul was pure evil. "Wait until you're called on," she snapped. "David, the answer?"

Mrs. Beak didn't know that David lived with a dino-head. "The answer?" he repeated, pretending for a moment that he didn't know. Then he let the Beak have it. "Of course. The cause of the extinction of the dinosaurs is not known. However, there are a number of theories. One is that the plant life changed and there wasn't food for the vegetarian dinosaurs to eat, which in turn meant there wasn't food for the meat-eaters. Another is that a giant volcano filled the sky with smoke, blocking out the sun and making the whole world too cold for the dinosaurs to survive. And there's the theory that a gigantic asteroid collided with the earth, having the same effect as a giant volcano. Or maybe it was just little green guys from outer space. . . ."

The angry spots of color in Mrs. Beak's cheeks deepened. "Are you trying to be funny, David?"

"No," said David.

Mrs. Beak turned on her heel and marched to the front of the room. "Open your books to page one twenty-six," she practically snarled.

"Good work, Dino-head," muttered Raul, keeping his head down as he flipped the pages of his book.

David knew better than to smile. But inside, he was deeply pleased with his victory. *Chalk one up for the dinosaurs,* he thought. *It's the revenge of the dino-heads.*

But not for long.

Mrs. Beak cleared her throat. "David. Since you know so much about dinosaurs, why don't you do a special report for the class."

"A special report?" David heard his voice go up in shock. He never, ever did special reports. Or work for extra credit. In subjects like science, he'd never needed to, at least until this year. And he wasn't interested enough in his other subjects to bother.

"Yessss," Mrs. Beak pressed, the little, mean, triumphant smile she usually wore returning to her lips. "And Raul?"

Raul, who'd been drilling a hole in his desk with his

pen and minding his own business, jumped a mile. "Uh, what was the question?"

"I think you'd better help David with his special report."

"Special report?" Raul's voice went up even more than David's had.

"Yes. No hurry. Tomorrow will be soon enough."

"Tomorrow! But—" Raul began.

"Page one twenty-six," Mrs. Beak said, ignoring Raul. "Polly, why don't you read for us, beginning at the top of the page."

As perfect Polly began to read in her singsong voice, David met Raul's eyes again.

In the war with Mrs. Beak, they'd just become prisoners.

"Mrs. Beak is nose slime," said Stacey as they walked out of Graveyard School. "Who let her become a schoolteacher?"

"Maybe she's not really a schoolteacher," suggested Maria. She pointed toward the old graveyard on the weedy hill behind the school. They all stared at it: rows and rows of crazily tilted, worn tombstones speckled with moss and lichen, separated from one edge of the playground by a jarringly white picket fence. A road cut through the middle of the graveyard and met another old road near the top. The school skateboard fanatics practiced up at the top of the hill. But even they avoided the graveyard and the road through it, just like everyone else in town. The graveyard was always empty. And the wind never seemed to stop whistling and moaning through the headstones.

"You're saying she's a ghost, come back to haunt us?" David asked.

Maria shrugged. "I'm saying I don't think she's human."

Stacey Carter said, "Well, we're stuck with her. I bet people have been complaining about her for years."

"I know they have," said Raul. "My brother had her. He warned me about her when I was back in first grade. Said if I was gonna get caught by a teacher breaking some school rule, not to get caught by her."

"You know what they say. The teacher isn't always right, but the teacher *is* always the teacher," cracked Stacey.

"Well, at least we have a hidden resource for our report," said Raul. He pointed at Richie, who was wandering down the steps toward them. He was reading. But somehow he never missed a step.

David and Raul both smiled big welcoming smiles as Richie came up to join them. Richie finally raised his head.

He stopped just out of reach. He stared at David. He stared at Raul.

"Uh-oh," he said.

But before he could make a break for it, Raul and David had each grabbed one of his arms. "C'mon, Reptileman," said David. "We've got work to do."

• • •

Richie spread his arms out. He dug his heels in. He pressed his back against the closed door of his room.

"No! No way!"

"C'mon, Richie," pleaded Raul. "We won't hurt it. We promise."

"Trust us," David added. He began to pry his brother's fingers from one side of the door frame.

"Moooom!" howled Richie.

"Okay, okay!" David quickly let go.

The three of them stood there, staring at one another. Then Raul said, "Richie, do you know who Mrs. Beak is? She's our science teacher. She's also the meanest, nastiest student-eating teacher in the entire world."

"She eats kids?" Richie said, looking alarmed.

"She would, if she'd thought of it," said David. "And she's out to get me. She hates me. And she says Raul and I have to have a report on dinosaurs by tomorrow."

"Or else," said Raul. He pretended to cut his throat with his finger.

Slowly Richie lowered his arms.

"All right!" David charged forward.

Richie threw his arms out again. "Wait a minute— *wait a minute.* I have rules."

"Right. Of course." David patted his brother's shoulder. "Just tell us the rules, Dino-he—er, Richie."

"You can have my dinotank for your report," said

Richie. "But you can't let *anyone* touch any of the dinosaurs. They're very picky. They don't like strangers."

"No problem," said David, catching Raul's eye and trying not to grin.

"And I have to visit them *every* day," Richie went on.

"If you want to voluntarily go in Mrs. Beak's class, be my guest," David said. "Just don't tell her it's your dinotank, okay?"

Richie looked scornful. "I know. . . . The third rule is, if anything happens to *any* of my dinosaurs or to my dinotank, you have to give me new dinosaurs and a new tank exactly the same."

"Done deal." David stuck out his hand.

He and Richie shook hands. Then Richie and Raul shook hands.

Richie turned, opened the door, and led the way to the tank. "You have to be very, very careful with the tank," he said.

"Can we borrow some of your dinosaur books?" said Raul. "To help write our report."

"Yeah—" Richie stopped so suddenly that Raul and David ran into him.

"Hey!" complained David.

Slowly Richie raised his arm. He pointed. "My tyrannosaurus!" he cried. "Trex! He's killed my alamosaurus!"

CHAPTER

5

David and Raul crowded around Richie to peer into the dinotank. At first David didn't notice anything unusual.

Then he saw it.

A small gray-green figure was lying on its side at the edge of the saucer pool. Its plastic head was almost totally ripped off its body. One front leg and one back leg were missing. The front leg was lying nearby.

"Wasn't that a brontosaurus or something?" asked Raul.

"That's the old name for the apatosaurus, which lived in the Jurassic Era," said Richie tearfully. "The alamosaurus lived during the Cretaceous Era, one of the few sauropods of that era. This is a *cretaceous* tank."

"Yeah, sure. I knew that," murmured Raul.

David kept staring at the mutilated alamosaurus.

"Wow," he said at last. "William really did a number on that guy."

"William! It wasn't William. It was Trex!" Richie shook his head sadly. "I knew I should have kept him separate from the other dinosaurs."

"Wait a minute, Richie. David's right. It *had* to be that killer cat of yours, right?" said Raul.

"I fixed the tank so William couldn't get in," Richie said.

Sure enough, the screen on top of the tank was still in place, weighted down with a dictionary and a volume of Richie's *Encyclopedia of Prehistoric Times.*

"William couldn't have done it, see? It was *him.*" Richie pointed toward the other end of the dinotank. Trex was standing near the cave. David frowned. The stupid plastic dinosaur looked bigger. And fatter.

No. It wasn't possible.

"Will's a crafty cat," said David, blinking hard. There, that was better. The stupid toy dinosaur hadn't gotten any bigger. The only thing that was getting bigger was Richie's imagination. And it was beginning to rub off on David.

Raul nudged David and pulled him to one side. "This is great," he whispered. "Dead, mutilated dinosaurs, the whole bit. *Very* realistic."

"I guess I'd better bury poor Alamo," said Richie.

"No! Wait!" Raul practically leaped back to Richie's side as Richie started to uncover the tank. "Can't we leave him?" asked Raul.

Looking startled and shocked, Richie cried, "No!" He paused. "Why?"

"Well, uh, uh, because if Trex killed him, then Trex needs to eat him. It's the dinosaur way, see? Like in the real Crustaceous Period."

"Cretaceous," said Richie. Slowly he nodded. "Perhaps you're right. I never thought of that before." He looked up at Raul. "Thank you."

"I'll tell you what," said David sympathetically. "We'll just borrow a couple of your dinosaur books for right now and go work on our report and leave you alone to say good-bye to Alamo."

Richie sighed and sat down in his chair by the dino-tank. He looked gratefully up at David and Raul.

"Glad to help," said David, refusing to meet Raul's eye.

A few minutes later, the two boys were staggering down the hall toward David's room under a load of dinosaur books. Raul had started laughing, and he was still laughing. "Your brother really is a dino-head," he panted. "I mean, he believes all that stuff is real."

"Yeah, yeah, yeah," said David. "But there's not much he doesn't know about them." He dropped his armload of books on his desk, while Raul let his stack slide onto David's bed. "It's a good thing there aren't any real dinosaurs around. He'd have run off to join them by now."

Raul said, "Too bad he can't give our report for us."

"Yeah." David grinned, envisioning the scene.

43

"Yeah. Dino-head and his dinosaurs would eat the Beak alive!"

Their report was a huge success—at least it was with everyone except Mrs. Beak. Her mouth dropped open when David and Raul staggered into her room before school, holding the dinotank.

"What's the meaning of this?" she demanded.

"Be careful!" Richie warned. He was holding two separate boxes, a small one with Trex in it and a larger one containing all the rest of the dinosaurs. He'd wrapped Alamo's remains separately in foil "so it wouldn't upset the other plant-eaters."

"It's a dinotank. For our dinosaur report. Where can we put it?" gasped David. Wordlessly, Mrs. Beak pointed to a vacant space on the shelf next to the lizard tank.

"Excellent," said Richie.

Mrs. Beak's eyes narrowed. "Who are you?"

"My brother," said David quickly. "We're letting him help."

Mrs. Beak gave Richie a suspicious look, but she didn't say anything else. She watched silently as the three of them assembled the dinotank.

Right, Mrs. Beak, thought David. *If you can't say something nasty, don't say anything at all.*

When they were finished, David gave Mrs. Beak a cheerful wave as they left the room. "See you in science class!" he said.

44

The report was superior. Even Mrs. Beak couldn't find any mistakes in it.

"It's nice to see you take your work seriously" was all she managed to say when David and Raul had finished.

The class crowded around the dinotank to study it.

"No touching," David warned.

"Euuuuuw!" shrieked Polly. "Look!" She pointed to Alamo's remains.

"Dinosaur dinner," said David.

Jaws said, "Yeah. I bet the dinosaurs were always hungry, too."

Polly shuddered. "I think it's *disgusting*. I don't think things like this should be allowed in class. It's very upsetting to someone as sensitive as I."

"Science is not pretty," said Mrs. Beak's soft, mean voice unexpectedly. The smile had returned to her face, as if the thought pleased her. "It's kill or be killed, eat or be eaten. For dinosaurs *and* for everyone else."

Mrs. Beak's soft, satisfied voice sent a chill down David's spine. Especially in combination with the realization that the remains of Alamo were much smaller than the day before.

Had Richie forgotten some dinosaur body part?

Or had Trex come back for another meal?

It took every ounce of will David had not to look down toward the cave at Trex, to see if the tiny toy dinosaur—which couldn't possibly have killed Alamo,

45

much less eaten him—had grown bigger since David had last seen him.

"David, how did your report go?"

David barely registered his mother's question. He'd been studying the chicken leg on his plate. Roast chicken. He usually liked it.

But something about it that night reminded him of—

"It went ballistic!" Richie said enthusiastically.

"It was nice of you to lend your brother your dino-tank," Mrs. Pike said to Richie. "Wasn't it, David? David?"

Tearing his attention away from the roast chicken leg, David quickly replayed in his mind the last sentences his mother had said.

"Yeah," he said at last. "Yeah, decent. Decent, Richie." He picked up the chicken leg gingerly.

Richie beamed. "I even let him take my alamosaurus that Trex killed, didn't I, David?"

"Ah, so your tyrannosaurus is killing other dinosaurs now, is it?" said Mr. Pike jovially.

The conversation around the dinner table once again faded from David's consciousness as he stared, riveted, at the chicken leg in his hand. Now he knew what it reminded him of.

He put the chicken leg down. "Could I have some more rice?" he said in a strangled voice.

No way was he gonna eat that chicken leg. Not tonight.

Not when it looked so much like the missing leg of the alamosaurus in the dinotank at school.

For some reason, when he fell asleep that night, David left his desk light on. He didn't know why he did it. But that was probably what woke him up much, much later.

That and the dream he'd been having: a dream of running through a ferny forest taller than he was. Of the *squish, squish, suck* of his feet slapping into the muddy, swampy ground.

Of something breathing nearby. Something big, breathing heavily.

Something with extremely bad breath. Breath that smelled like rotting meat.

He opened his eyes and escaped from his dream with relief—until he saw the shadow of the giant dinosaur head on the wall and the bright flash of white light that suddenly filled his room.

Too shocked to be frightened, David bolted upright in his bed. He blinked, dots from the blinding light dancing in front of his eyes.

When he looked again, the shadow was gone.

But crashing sounds were coming from outside his window. Still half blinded, David jumped out of bed and stumbled over to the window.

An odd voice speaking a strange, whistling sort of

language rose agitatedly through the dark. Or was it someone whistling for their dog? Was that it?

An enormous dark form seemed to fill the yard. The voices became more agitated. Were there figures, kid-sized figures, moving around below?

David rubbed his eyes and leaned forward. But suddenly there was another blinding flash of light, a crash, and an enormous whoosh of wind, like the tail-lash of an angry tornado.

In spite of himself, David jumped back, holding his hands up defensively.

Nothing else happened.

Carefully David edged toward the window again. He looked out. But the night was quiet and very dark.

Whatever had been crashing around down below was gone.

CHAPTER

6

Breakfast was on the table. The automatic coffee-maker was making coffee. The kitchen was deserted. The back door was open.

For one awful, sleepy moment, David thought his entire family had been abducted by aliens.

Then he heard his father's voice outside the kitchen door. "I didn't even hear anything, did you?"

His mother's voice said something David couldn't quite hear. But she sounded upset.

"Mom? Dad?" David walked out the back door and stopped.

The huge cedar tree in the middle of the backyard no longer stood where it always had. Instead it lay, split in half, its roots torn out of the ground, a hurricane litter of branches and leaves all around it.

"Maybe it was lightning," said Mrs. Pike.

"Maybe," answered their father dubiously.

"Wow," breathed David. "Wipeout." Was that what

he had seen and heard last night? Some weird flash of lightning striking the old tree?

Maybe, he thought.

Hearing David, his parents turned. "I'm afraid so," said his father. "Completely destroyed. I couldn't have done it better with a bulldozer."

His mother said, "Well, we can cut up the wood and use it for something, even if it's only for firewood. . . . Let's go get breakfast or we're all gonna be late this morning."

David turned. His little brother was standing in the kitchen doorway, his eyes wide.

"Hey, Reptileman, what's up?" said David.

Richie clutched David's sleeve. "We have to go to school," he said.

"Yeah, but it's almost the weekend," David said consolingly. He headed for the orange juice.

But Richie still held on to David's sleeve.

"Hello, Richie? You can let go now," David said.

"We have to go to school *right now,*" Richie said.

"What?"

Richie didn't answer. He ran back into the house. A minute later, just as David was sitting down at the breakfast table with his mom and dad, Richie rushed back in, holding his backpack.

"I have to get to school early today," he gasped. "I forgot. It's for . . . a project."

Mr. Pike put down his fork. "Want me to drive you, son?"

"Uh, no. I'll just hurry."

"Not by yourself you won't," Mrs. Pike said firmly.

"David can go with me now. Can't you, David?" Richie fixed his gaze on his brother.

"I haven't even finished my breakfast," David complained.

"Please?" said Richie.

"You haven't had any breakfast at all, Richie," Mrs. Pike objected.

Richie grabbed a bagel off the table and stuffed a hunk of it in his mouth. "Can we go now?" he pleaded with David, somewhat thickly.

"All right, all right." David threw his napkin down and went to get his own backpack. Returning to the kitchen, he grabbed a bagel for himself and spread jam on it.

He went to join Richie, who was dancing by the kitchen door like a spark coming up off a fire.

"Bye!" shrieked Richie, and ran.

"See ya," David said to the two puzzled Pike parents, and took off after his brother.

"Hey, Scrambled Eggs for Brains, slow down!" David called.

Richie slowed down. Slightly.

David broke into a run and caught up with him. "How can you run and eat a bagel at the same time?"

"Bagel?" Richie looked down at the bagel he held in his hand, a huge bite gone from one side. "You want it?"

"No. And don't take off again!" David made a last-minute save, catching Richie by the edge of his jean jacket. "Slow down and tell me what's going on."

"We have to *hurry!*" cried Richie.

"We're hurrying. We're going to get to school early." David shuddered at the thought. "And I'm not going any faster than this, especially if you don't tell me what the deal is."

Still pulling against David's grip, Richie said, "Don't you get it? It wasn't lightning or wind that knocked that tree over . . . it was a dinosaur."

David stopped dead. "That does it. You've completely lost it now, Richie."

"It was," said Richie. "I know it was. . . . I should never have let you have the dinotank. . . . Maybe it was one of my dinosaurs, trying to get back home."

Poor kid, thought David. *He really does believe it. And he sounds like he's completely lost his mind.*

He started walking again, still holding on to Richie with one hand. He took another bite of bagel and chewed thoughtfully.

"Okay, okay," he said at last. "We'll go up to the school and check it out. But I gotta tell you, Richie, you're completely out of your cranium on this one."

Richie didn't answer. He pulled against David's hold and David let go. Richie took off.

With a sigh, David started jogging after his little brother so that he could keep him in sight until they reached Graveyard School.

It was so early that there were no cars in the teachers' parking lot.

"See? No dinosaurs," said David, coming up beside Richie, who had skidded to a halt on the road in front of the school.

"I don't understand," Richie muttered, almost to himself. He started forward.

David made another grab and caught Richie's arm. "Whoa. Where ya going now?"

"Around back."

"Well, you can't just go, like, circling the school at dawn . . . it looks weird. Suppose someone saw us? Suppose Dr. Morthouse came extra early?"

The effect of the principal's name was a powerful one. Richie stopped in his tracks. "What should we do?"

"We, uh—we check it out. Low-profile. Like this."

David led the way down the road to where the scrubby woods behind the fence at the edge of the schoolyard began. He crouched down. "Follow me," he whispered. He didn't know why he whispered, since there was no one around to hear him.

"Check," Richie whispered back.

Keeping low, they went all the way down the fence and around the back of the school, standing up slowly from time to time to take a look at the school. Each time, the school looked the same, except better lit as the morning grew brighter.

Until they reached the corner where the wire fence met the picket fence that separated the lower edge of the graveyard from Graveyard School.

David hesitated. He didn't like the idea of walking around in the graveyard, even the edge of the graveyard, even during daylight. Too many strange things had been seen there. Too many bizarre events had happened.

He'd heard about a lot of them. But he was sure there were a lot more that he hadn't heard about.

"David, what's wrong? Do you see anything?" Richie's voice sounded excited. David could tell he was really getting into spying on the school.

David sighed. He looked up the hill at the crazily tilted, weatherworn graves. The morning sun made the stones cast a crazy quilt of shadows over the uneven ground. They didn't look particularly scary right at the moment.

They're just graves, he told himself. *You have to believe in ghosts for them to get you.*

And he didn't believe in ghosts. He didn't even believe in dinosaurs.

"C'mon," David said.

They crept along the picket fence. In spite of himself, David kept casting quick, uneasy looks over at the graves, which were suddenly very, very close.

"David!" Richie almost shrieked, although he was whispering.

David jumped a mile. He whirled and grabbed Richie.

Richie grabbed him.

David started to run.

Richie held on. "David, look!"

David realized that it wasn't fear in his little brother's voice, it was excitement. Slowly he turned.

And instinctively ducked low, grabbing Richie and pulling him down with him. The two boys lay flat on their stomachs and peered across the dirt and grass at the back door of Graveyard School.

Or what used to be the back door. Now both doors had been thrown outward, as if a blast had come from inside the school. Huge, splintery gashes ran down the doors, which were pitched out onto the grass like a couple of playing cards someone had thrown down.

"Whoaaaa," breathed David.

"See?" said Richie, suddenly sounding pleased and a little smug. "See? I told you! Dinosaurs."

"Dinosaurs?" asked David. "I don't see any dinosaurs, Rich. What I do see is Basement Bart. And he looks like he could take on a tyrannosaurus and win."

Sure enough, Basement Bart had emerged from the darkened depths of the school through the hole where the doors had been. He walked out into the schoolyard and turned to face the school. He put his hands on his hips.

For a long time, he didn't move. He just stood there, dressed as usual in a green army camouflage shirt, faded overalls, and enormous workboots. His gray-streaked hair was, as usual, pulled back in a ponytail. And as usual, even standing still, he looked enormous—and menacing.

Suddenly Basement Bart turned. He stared up the hill at the graveyard. He seemed to be studying it, as if he was looking for whoever had blasted the doors off the building. He lowered his searching gaze. Now he seemed to be staring at the picket fence.

He seemed to be staring at them.

David turned his head slightly and breathed into Richie's ear, "Be ready to run."

For a long, long moment, they lay there, trying to mash themselves into invisibility behind the fence.

Then, so abruptly that it made them both jump, Basement Bart swung back around. He strode around the side of the building and opened a door that led into the basement.

"C'mon!" said Richie. He bounced to his feet.

"What are you doing now?" David whispered.

"We've got to go see what happened. We've got to get inside the school before anyone else comes along."

David made another grab for his insane little brother. But this time he was too late.

Richie had raced down the fence to the gate, had pushed through, and was heading at top speed for the jagged, gaping hole in the back of Graveyard School.

CHAPTER
7

"Richie, wait!" David called as loudly as he dared.

Richie ignored him.

David stood up. He looked wildly around. He almost wished something would come up out of the graveyard. Almost anything would be better than chasing his dumb little brother into the school and getting trapped there with Basement Bart.

But no ghosts or ghouls came to his rescue.

David started running after his brother.

Was it his imagination, or did he hear Bart's basement door opening as he raced up the back steps? The sound of a car pulling into the teachers' parking lot?

He ran into the shadowy building and skidded to a halt, breathing hard. Most of the lights were off, but it was easy to see that something terrible had happened.

Lockers on either side of the walls had been randomly smashed and bashed. Notebooks and books that had spilled out had been scattered and torn.

Chunks of plaster lay on the floor. David looked up. There were dents and gouges in the ceiling . . . as if something had walked along bumping its head.

David was suddenly afraid. It wasn't possible. He knew it couldn't be true.

But what if his little brother had run straight into the jaws of a waiting *Tyrannosaurus rex*?

David did not hesitate this time. He took off. He ran down the hall, following the trail of debris.

Fortunately, he didn't have far to go. The trail led straight to Mrs. Beak's room.

The door to Mrs. Beak's room stopped him for a moment. It wasn't closed. It just wasn't there. He turned his head and saw it halfway down the hall, the glass in the top half completely blown away.

"Richie," he said softly.

"In here," said Richie, his voice excited.

Stepping carefully now to avoid the glass, David went into Mrs. Beak's room.

Desks were overturned and books were flung everywhere.

Richie was crouched in the corner. As David drew nearer, he saw Richie's dinotank. It was lying in a twisted, shattered heap on its side on the floor.

"Your dinotank!" said David.

"They're not all gone," said Richie. "Look." He held up his hand. Tiny dinosaurs lay in his palm.

"Who's missing?" asked David, forgetting that he hadn't believed Richie, forgetting that he didn't believe it was possible for the dinosaurs to come back.

Richie looked up solemnly. "Trex," he said, softly. "Trex is gone. He's the only one."

David swallowed hard. "He . . . came to life and got big enough to . . ." He looked wildly around. "Why didn't he just go out the window?"

"I think he wasn't thinking about escape," said Richie. "I think he was thinking about dinner. Look."

David looked. The lizard tank was smashed on the floor, too. "The lizard got out and Trex chased him?"

"Yep," Richie said. "Maybe the lizard got under the door and Trex tried to follow him. And then when he got out in the dark hall, he just headed toward the light."

David met Richie's eyes. "Trex is a *Tyrannosaurus rex,* right?"

Richie nodded.

"And they grow"—David searched his mind for the facts from his report—"up to forty feet, and weigh up to ten tons."

Richie nodded again.

"With serrated teeth, like a steak knife, uh, seven inches long."

Richie nodded again.

"And they eat meat."

"Yeah," said Richie. "They eat meat. . . . *T. rex* was the most fearsome predator that *ever* lived."

"Aha!" shrieked a fearsome, evil voice.

Before David and Richie knew what had happened, Mrs. Beak was upon them. She grabbed them by their arms and jerked them upright. "Gotcha!"

"M-Mrs. Beak!" David said. "What're you doing here?"

"I teach here," said Mrs. Beak. She then asked, very, very softly, "And what, might I ask, are you two doing in my classroom?"

Her voice was so soft and so evil that David and Richie both cringed.

Mrs. Beak looked around the trashed classroom. "Or maybe that's a question I don't need to ask."

"We got here early and the back door was . . . open," said David. "We saw what had happened and we came inside to, to . . ."

"To make sure no one was hurt," Richie said. "You see, Trex—"

"A likely story," Mrs. Beak interrupted. "When Dr. Morthouse and I are through with you—"

"But my dinosaur! Trex! He's escaped! You don't understand!"

Mrs. Beak bent down until her pale blue, deeply mean eyes were close to Richie's terrified brown ones. "You listen to me. The dinosaurs are extinct, gone, kaput. And you know why? Because they're stupid, that's why. They deserve to be extinct!"

Richie's mouth dropped open in shock. David saw

anger replace the fear in his little brother's eyes. "They do not!" Richie shouted. "Let me go!"

"Oh, no," purred Mrs. Beak, straightening up. "All your crazy stories won't get you out of this mess, young man. You and your big brother—"

"Might as well let 'em go. Door was open."

Slowly, as if he were in a bad dream, David turned his head. Basement Bart was standing there. And he had spoken!

David had known Basement Bart could talk. Other kids had heard him. Had even talked to him. But not David.

"Mess was already made before they got here. Happened last night."

"How do you know, Mr. Bartholomew?" Mrs. Beak demanded.

"I know," said Basement Bart.

The two stared at each other for a long moment. Then Mrs. Beak said, "Very well. You may go. But I've got my eye on you both, remember that."

She gave both David and Richie one last quick shake and let them go.

"We're outta here," said David. "C'mon!"

He was out the door and down the hall before he realized that Richie wasn't with him.

He spun around. Richie had stopped in the doorway of Mrs. Beak's classroom. He was looking up at Basement Bart.

"Thank you," David heard him say.

Basement Bart didn't answer.

"Richie!" David said.

But Richie wasn't through yet. "Mr. Bartholomew," he said. "Have you seen Trex? Have you seen my dinosaur?"

This time Basement Bart did answer. "Good luck, kid," he said. He turned and walked away.

"Attention, students! Attention!"

Mr. Hannibal Lucre, the assistant principal, stood at the microphone at the front of the auditorium. "Attention!"

The noise got louder and louder. An emergency assembly had been called before school could even begin. The students were packed into the auditorium every which way: For the first time in the history of the school, the first graders weren't lined neatly up in the rows down front, with the other classes in ascending order behind them.

"Awesome!" shouted Raul to David above the din.

"Didja *see* the door to the boys' bathroom? Completely smashed in!" Maria told Stacey and Polly.

"Grossssss!" shrieked Polly, covering her eyes as if she were actually looking into the boys' bathroom.

"Attention!" Mr. Lucre pleaded, rubbing his plump hands together.

David was the only one who wasn't talking.

Except maybe Richie, wherever he was.

"Be quiet," said a firm voice.

Absolute silence fell over the auditorium as Dr. Morthouse took the microphone from Mr. Lucre. "Thank you, Mr. Lucre," she said. "It seems the students are a little upset. Otherwise, I'm sure you boys and girls wouldn't be so rude. Would you?"

Such was the power of Dr. Morthouse that some of the students actually answered, "No, Dr. Morthouse."

And no one even giggled.

"We've had a slight problem, as you know, here at our beloved school," Dr. Morthouse went on. "But with our capable, er, school cleaning engineer, Mr. Bartholomew, who has brought in additional help, I'm sure we will soon have everything under control. In the meanwhile, we have made certain alternate arrangements: Mrs. Beak's class will meet in here for the morning, at least, until the classroom is straightened up. Those students whose lockers . . ."

Something made David look out the windows on the far wall of the auditorium. Through them he could see the old graveyard. He didn't know why he looked. He'd had about enough of that old graveyard today. He'd had about enough of everything.

But staring out windows was a hard habit to break, even when there was a remote possibility that Dr. Morthouse would catch him in the act.

Dr. Morthouse droned on. David stared, not really seeing anything, trying to think.

Then his brain identified what his eyes had been watching.

An odd-shaped hump at the very top of the hill. A hump that he had never seen there before.

A gray-green, mossy-colored hump.

Even as David watched, the hump began to move. Huge saber-clawed feet stretched out and began to push forward. The thing raised an enormous, lizardlike head.

"No," said David softly.

Other heads turned. A deathly silence fell over the auditorium.

Then a familiar voice rang out: "There he is! My dinosaur! Trex!"

CHAPTER
8

"Aaaaaaaaah!" screamed a voice that sounded like Polly Hannah's. "Help! We'll all be killed."

"Sit down this instant!" Dr. Morthouse bellowed.

Mr. Lucre began to wring his hands. "Girls and boys, boys and girls!" he wailed.

But it was no use. Panicked kids raced for the doors. Panicked teachers tried to avoid being trampled.

David fought his way toward Richie, who was leading a small group of students to the windows.

"Wait!" Richie was calling. "Trex! It's me!"

Richie flung himself at the window and began trying to pry it open. It rose a crack. Richie pressed his lips to the crack and shouted in his thin, reedy voice, *"Trex! Trex!"*

For a moment, David thought he saw the huge dinosaur head turn toward the school.

It made his blood run cold. How could Richie think that big monster was his friend?

Trex wasn't Richie's friend. Trex was trying to decide whether the sound of Richie's voice was the sound of his breakfast calling.

Then the dinosaur turned his head away. And as suddenly as he had appeared, he was gone.

The doors of the auditorium, which had been closed, had held up against the assault of the panicked students.

And Dr. Morthouse had come down off the stage to stride through the middle of the chaos. "Knock it off!" she snarled, grabbing students left and right, giving them a good shake. "Quit acting like babies. Sit down in your seats! You sixth graders look like wimps! Sit down!"

Under the cover of the noise and confusion, David grabbed Richie and yanked him away from the window. He shoved his wild-eyed little brother into the nearest seat and sat down next to him.

"Shut up!" he said.

"But David, it was Trex. He saw me! He knew me!"

"He wanted to eat you, you little twerp!"

"He did not!" Richie bounced indignantly up out of his chair.

David dragged him back down again.

"Sit down! If they figure out you started all this, Dr. Morthouse is going to rip off your head. And you'll wish it was just a *T. rex* after you."

"But—"

"We'll find him, okay?" David promised wildly. Anything to get his deranged brother to be quiet. "I swear."

"Cross your heart and hope to die?" chanted Richie.

"Yes, yes, *yes!* Now be quiet."

Richie was quiet.

Meanwhile, as Dr. Morthouse waded through the sea of students, laying down the law, Mr. Lucre had seized the microphone.

"It's gone," Mr. Lucre whinnied in terror. "Not that it was ever there, but it's gone, boys and girls."

Gradually order was restored.

Dr. Morthouse marched back to the mike and snatched it from Mr. Lucre.

"Sit. Down. Now!" she roared.

Everyone who was still standing sat.

"Be. Quiet."

Someone giggled once, nervously. The sound died away.

Dr. Morthouse glared down at the student body of Graveyard School.

The student body stared back.

"Whoever started this . . . this joke . . . will *pay.* Do I make myself clear?"

David looked over at Richie. Did the kid understand just how much trouble he was in?

Trouble? What about the dinosaur? Good grief.

There was a real live dinosaur out there.

Something so big, so mean that not even Dr. Morthouse could face it and live.

And he'd promised his little brother he'd help him find it.

David groaned and buried his face in his hands. The day had started out badly and gotten worse.

He hated to imagine how it was going to end.

"Vandalism at Grove Hill school. What is this world coming to!" Mrs. Hannah shook her head. Polly shook her head, too, so vigorously that her yellow curls bounced.

"Get in the car, Polly."

"Can we go shopping, Mother?" Polly whined as she climbed into the front seat of her mother's car. "I got an *ugly* smudge on my skirt when everybody was pretending they saw the dinosaur."

"A smudge!" Mrs. Hannah shook her head even harder. "What is this world coming—" Her voice was cut off as the door of the car slammed shut.

David and Richie watched the car speed away. All around them, parents were driving up to the front door of the school and loading their kids in. Other kids were getting on bicycles under the agitated gaze of Mr. Lucre. "Calmly, calmly, there's no need to panic," Mr. Lucre was muttering. He kept waving his arms like a traffic cop gone berserk.

The kids ignored him. But they behaved. There were too many parents around. Also, Dr. Morthouse was standing at the top of the steps by the front door, scowling at everyone.

For the first time any of the kids could remember, Grove Hill Elementary School was closing early. Although Dr. Morthouse had declared the dinosaur sighting a practical joke, near-hysteria had nevertheless taken over the school and the teachers had found teaching class impossible. Just before lunch, Dr. Morthouse had announced on the loudspeaker that school was closed. The school bus was on its way, parents were being notified, and the announcement was being made on the radio and the television and all over the town of Grove Hill.

No one had been disappointed, except possibly Jaws Bennett. "I'm going to miss lunch," he'd complained.

He'd gotten no sympathy.

Remembering what Jaws had said, David realized that it was lunchtime. He was hungry.

He thought about Trex. Trex was probably hungry, too. And Trex's appetite was probably much bigger than even someone like Jaws. Much, *much* bigger.

That took care of David's appetite. He wasn't hungry anymore.

Feeling Dr. Morthouse's eyes upon him, David bent over and said into Richie's ear, "Here comes Dad. Be cool. Don't talk about anything. That way he won't be suspicious and we can come back and, uh, track Trex. Okay?"

David waved at Raul, who was talking to some kids nearby. "C'mon!" he called. "Dad's here."

Raul trotted over and the three of them got into the car.

"Quite an exciting day, eh?" asked Mr. Pike, pulling away from the school.

"Super!" said Raul. "Hey. You should've thought of that dinosaur gag sooner, Richoman."

Quickly David said, "Richie just imagined that. It was someone's idea of a practical joke and it . . . it scared him."

"I wasn't scared!" Richie spoke up indignantly. "I—" He caught David's warning look and said, "I . . . was just upset about my dinotank getting messed up."

"Yeah?" Mr. Pike asked.

David took the lead. "Yeah. Whoever broke into the school last night trashed the dinotank. Smithereens. Glass confetti. Wipeout."

Raul hadn't seen the tank. His attention was diverted from the topic of the dinosaur. "Tough luck, Richie. I didn't know. Your dinosaurs, did they, uh, make it?"

Richie opened his mouth. David made a warning face.

Swallowing hard, Richie said, "No."

"Awesome day," said Raul. Then he frowned. "What do you think you saw out that window, anyway, Richie?"

With his eyes fastened on David, Richie shrugged. David nodded slightly. *Good.*

Raul looked suspicious now. Fortunately, they'd

reached his house. "Here we are," said Mr. Pike, as if Raul didn't know what his own house looked like.

David rolled his eyes at Raul and Raul grinned. "Thanks, Mr. Pike," he said. He got out of the car and looked back at Richie. The suspicious look returned to his face. "So, I'll talk to you later, Brother of Dinohead," he said to David.

"Sure," said David casually. He waved as if it was no big deal.

At the house, their father said, "You boys want to talk about what happened or anything? I mean . . ." His voice trailed off.

"Nope," said Richie. "I want a new dinotank. Could we talk about that?"

Mr. Pike smiled and ruffled Richie's hair. "We'll discuss it over dinner. When your mother gets home," he promised.

David said, "Can we wait to start our homework until later, Dad?"

"I don't see why not," said Mr. Pike. He looked at his watch, then glanced toward his study door. "What are you planning on doing until then?"

It was David's turn to shrug. "Bike around. You know."

"Hang out," said Richie urgently.

Their father shook his head and laughed. His thoughts were clearly still on his work, behind the study door.

"Don't let us bother you, Dad," said David.

"Fine," said Mr. Pike absently.

The two boys waited until their father was safely in the study.

"Dump your books and let's go," David said in a hoarse whisper. The two boys raced through the house, and a few minutes later they were pedaling their bikes as fast as they could back up the road to Graveyard School.

The school looked deserted.

"Wow," said Richie. "Everybody's left. It's like a science fiction movie or something."

"Try nightmare," David muttered. He waved his brother to a stop. "Remember, Basement Bart's probably still around. We better go the back way, take the Skateboard Hill road." He turned left onto Grove Road, the road that ran in front of the school, and headed away from the school and the town of Grove Hill.

It seemed to take forever to reach the turn onto Skateboard Hill. The road was an old farm road that wasn't used anymore. It led by gradual loops and curves through woods and overgrown pastures to the top of the hill behind the old graveyard. It wasn't really named Skateboard Hill. But everyone called it that because it was the best skateboarding place around town.

Although some people said it was haunted.

David decided not to think about that as he pedaled

his bike up Skateboard Hill. It was the middle of the day and ghosts usually did their ghost thing at midnight, he reasoned. Besides, he had bigger things to worry about. Much bigger things.

Unless Dr. Morthouse had been right. Unless the whole thing, the dinosaur sighting, the trashing of the school building, was part of some huge, dumb practical joke that had gotten out of hand. And the dinosaur sighting had been a sort of mass hallucination brought on by the power of suggestion.

She'd said something like that, anyway. It had sounded good. David wasn't in any position to argue. He was too busy trying to keep Richie quiet so that no one would remember that Richie was the one who'd started the dinosaur stampede in the auditorium.

Maybe it had been a mass hallucination—everybody imagining they were seeing the same thing at the same time. People's eyes could play tricks on them. Look at magicians. They did it all the time, made people believe that coins could disappear and humans could float in thin air.

They'd reached the top of the hill at last. David pulled his bike to the side of the road and let it drop. Richie did the same. The landscape below them was woods and trees and farmland. Behind them was where the road they called Skateboard Hill began—or ended.

Graveyard School sat at the foot of the steep hill, its back doors boarded shut now. Then came the white picket fence, sharp and shiny and new-looking. Then the old tombstones, worn and rounded, divided by the sharply bending road known as Deadman's Curve.

Rumor had it that there was a grave somewhere in the graveyard that glowed in the dark. . . .

David cleared his throat and turned his back on the less than picture-perfect scenery. "Is this where you think you saw the dinosaur?"

"Trex was back there," said Richie, ignoring the doubt in his older brother's voice. He pointed up the grassy slope of the hill toward the woods where the road ended.

"Okay," said David. "But listen, Rich, maybe it wasn't a dinosaur. Maybe it was just a shadow. You know. Or some dumb joke, like Dr. Morthouse sa—"

David didn't finish his sentence. He'd tripped and fallen forward. Hard. Facedown onto hard-packed dirt.

"Hey!"

Scrambling up, David turned to face his brother. "What happened?"

Richie pointed down at David's feet. "Look!" he said. "Look, David."

David looked. He didn't like what he saw. It made the hair on his neck stand up. It made chillbumps crawl up his arms.

He was standing in a giant footprint. A giant, clawed footprint.

The footprint of a dinosaur. A killer dinosaur named Trex.

CHAPTER

9

"He went that way!" said Richie, waving his arm.

Trying to remain calm, David stepped out of the giant footprint. Footprints could be faked, he told himself. Look at all the fake footprints of Bigfoot people were always "discovering."

He turned to face where Richie was pointing. The road that led back into the woods had always been overgrown. Blocked with fallen trees and tangles of wild blackberry and blueberry bushes and all kinds of still living trees.

Until today. Now it was clear. You could have driven a Mack truck down the road into the woods.

Or a dinosaur.

"Geez," David muttered. "It's true." It was true. The dinosaur was real.

But how? How could it have come to life?

"What's on the other side of the hill?" Richie asked, interrupting David's thoughts.

"I don't know. I've never been on the other side of the hill," said David. "I've never even *thought* about the other side of the hill." He didn't add that he'd had trouble enough on this side of the hill.

"I hope there aren't any highways or anything," Richie was saying worriedly. "What if he got hit by a car?"

"Don't worry. He wouldn't feel it."

Reluctantly, David started forward. Then he stopped. "Look, we can't just follow this guy into the woods. We've gotta get a map or something. Maybe we can, you know, figure out where this guy is going. And maybe, if we can figure out how this all happened . . . we can, uh, you know, stop him."

Richie looked suspicious. "Stop him how?"

"I don't know. One thing at a time, okay?"

"You better not hurt my dinosaur!"

"I won't. I promise." David thought hard. "We could check the glove compartment of the car. Maybe there's a map of Grove Hill in there. Or at a service station."

"The library," suggested Richie.

"Yeah. Good. C'mon. Let's go. We've got a lot of work to do."

"I hope Trex is smart enough to stay out of sight," Richie said, getting on his bike and pedaling after his brother.

David didn't answer. What could he say?

"Of course, maybe the *Tyrannosaurus rex* only

likes to hunt at night. Like cats, you know? And sharks. Sharks are most active at night, did you know that?"

Again David didn't answer. He just kept biking as fast as he could. And keeping his eyes peeled for any hungry tyrannosauruses.

Just in case they didn't only hunt at night.

"A map of Grove Hill?" the librarian said. "Why?"

"For a school project," said David, elbowing his little brother before Richie could volunteer any embarrassing, attention-getting information.

"How nice. You get out of school early and start right in on your schoolwork." The librarian smiled at them approvingly. It was an okay smile. Not like the ones the adults generally handed out at Graveyard School, David decided. He liked her, too, because she didn't start talking about school getting out early, asking a lot of questions. She was a cool librarian. And really tall, too. David wondered if she played basketball. He wondered if being tall helped her in her job, reaching the books up on the top shelves . . .

". . . over there," said the librarian, pointing.

Richie tugged at David's sleeve.

David gave her his best good-student smile back. "Thanks," he said.

The librarian smiled again. "You know, I've applied for a job at your school. They're looking for a librarian, did you know that?"

"No. Cool," said David. "Er, good luck."

He didn't add that he didn't think the school was going to be around much longer. Not if it had any more close encounters of the dinosaur kind.

He and Richie went over to the shelves where the librarian had directed them. Soon they were studying a map of Grove Hill.

"There it is," said Richie. "There's Graveyard School. Look, it has the road and the graveyard and everything!"

They both bent forward. "Look!" Richie went on. "Skateboard Hill used to be Landings Road. Isn't that funny? What does that mean?"

"Probably some old farmer's name, or something," said David absently. He was tracing the line that was Skateboard Hill up into the woods. There the road turned into a series of dots. "No longer in use," the map said. The dots led over the hill and then stopped abruptly.

"A swamp! A swamp!" Richie cried.

People turned and looked. The librarian did, too. She raised one finger to her lips with a little smile.

David nodded and turned back around. "Will you keep it *down*? You're going to get us thrown out!"

"A swamp," Richie repeated in a more normal voice.

"Go on," said David.

"They lived in swamplike areas. I mean, they think, the scientists, that the whole world was kinda swampy, you know? I bet that's where Trex is heading. For the swamp. Like by instinct. Isn't he smart?"

"He's not a pet dog, Richie," David said. "He's a big, alamosaurus-eating dinosaur. To him, we're junk food. Snacks."

He might as well have been talking to a wall. Richie's eyes were shining with anticipation.

"He'll be safe in the swamp. Nobody ever goes into swamps, right? 'Cause they're full of snakes and alligators and things."

"Mosquitoes, too," said David sarcastically. "Don't forget the mosquitoes."

He hoped his little brother was right.

Or maybe he didn't.

He wasn't sure he wanted to spend any time at all in a swamp. Especially not a swamp that had a hungry *T. rex* living in it.

"What do we do now?" asked Richie.

"You tell me, Dino-head." David closed the book and put it back. "One thing we do is get home. Dad's expecting us."

He thought Richie would argue, but Richie surprised him. He fell into step obediently.

"You're right," he told David. "We can't go look for Trex now. He's probably sleeping or something. We should wait until tonight, when he's most active. Early evening would be best, or early morning, I think."

David said firmly, "We can't go dinosaur hunting in the early evening. How would we explain why we weren't, like, eating dinner? And doing homework? Mom and Dad would notice we were missing for sure."

"Okay. We'll go early in the morning. Before sunrise." Richie gave a little skip of what looked like pure happiness, while David groaned inwardly. But all David said aloud was "Before sunrise. Yeah. Well, at least we know how to find out when that happens."

"How?"

"Dad's an astronomer, right? He ought to know the answer to that," David said.

David was right. Sort of. When they got home, their father was just bending over to pick up the newspaper off the front stoop. The paperboy, a new kid in school named Algie, was disappearing down the street.

"That's some arm that kid's got," their father said admiringly, watching Algie pedal away.

"Yeah," David said impatiently. He didn't know Algie well, just that he hung out with Kirstin Bjorg and kids like that. Kirstin was class president and the sort of student teachers described as "having a good head on her shoulders." None of which interested David.

"Dad, listen," David said. "What time does the sun rise tomorrow morning?"

Their father was studying the newspaper now. "Hmm? Sunrise? Tomorrow? Six-oh-eight A.M. exactly."

Shooting a triumphant look at Richie, David said, "Thanks, Dad."

"No problem."

"How'd you know that, Dad? Huh? How?" Richie said. "Do all astronomers know stuff like that?"

Their father looked up from the paper and grinned. "Nah," he said. "It's right here, see? Printed in the newspaper weather forecast."

Laughing, Mr. Pike went back into the house.

Richie started laughing, too.

Disgusted, David said, "Well, he knew the answer, didn't he?" He went into the house to try to take his mind off his troubles with something really radical: homework.

The light was blinding. The creatures from outer space were shooting lasers into his brain. He couldn't see. He was going to die. . . .

David sat up in bed with a jerk.

"Are you awake?" asked Richie, shining his flashlight directly in his older brother's eyes.

"No, I'm dead," David said sarcastically.

"It's time to get up," Richie said.

"Duh," said David. He slid off the bed and pulled on his shoes. He'd fallen asleep with his clothes on.

He hadn't planned to fall asleep at all. In fact, not falling asleep was the only plan he had.

So far, I'm not doing so good, thought David.

He finished knotting his shoelaces and reached up and snatched the flashlight out of Richie's hands.

"Hey," Richie protested.

Pulling on a dark jacket and a dark cap, David turned

to inspect his brother. Like David, Richie was dressed in jeans, black high-tops, and a dark T-shirt. He had on a dark hooded sweatshirt.

"How well can these *T. rexes* see in the dark?" asked David.

Richie shrugged. David realized that his little brother was clutching a box. "What's that?"

"The box Trex came in."

Even as Richie spoke, David recognized the box with all its instructions stamped on the outside: THIS SIDE UP. HANDLE WITH CARE. FRAGILE. DO NOT EXPOSE TO HEAT OR COLD. DO NOT EXPOSE TO HIGH-INTENSITY LIGHT.

"Ha," said David sourly. "You couldn't even fit one of his teeth in there! What're you going to do, say some magic words and make him shrink back down to size?"

"You got a better idea?" Richie said.

"Shhh! Yeah, leave the box, Lizard Brain."

"But—"

"Leave it or I'm quitting right now."

Reluctantly Richie put the box down. David flicked off the flashlight. "Let's go," he said. He sounded braver than he felt. Lots braver. "Let's go hunt dinosaurs."

They reached the top of Graveyard Hill in no time at all. David pushed his bike to the edge of the trees and hid it. Wordlessly, Richie did the same.

The night was still dark. But even as they stepped

into the dark tunnel of road that Trex had made, a bird began to sing sleepily.

The two boys walked slowly into the woods.

For a while the road went steadily uphill. David kept the flashlight on, but he held it low and pointed the circle of light close to their feet. He didn't want to attract any unnecessary attention.

More birds woke up and began to sing.

The woods grew lighter. Trunks of trees began to emerge from the darkness. Branches. Fallen logs.

They reached the top of the hill and began to go down the other side.

The going was harder now, as if there had never been a road to follow. They had to scramble over tree trunks or climb under big branches. Rocks rolled away under their feet, and matted leaves and underbrush made it hard for them to keep from slipping.

David didn't even realize that they'd reached the edge of the swamp until Richie gave a muffled scream.

"Shhh!" David said automatically, grabbing his little brother and yanking him back.

"I stepped in some water," said Richie.

David looked up. Tall reeds were growing all around them. The path the dinosaur had cut through the woods was now a sort of flattened highway through the tall, tall grass. Beneath them, the ground became muddy. It made hungry, sucking noises against their high-tops as they walked. The morning call of birds was joined by the whine of insects.

"Oww!" muttered David, slapping at something that had bitten him.

"We're lucky it's not summer," Richie said. "Then there'd be about a trillion more insects."

"I'm celebrating," said David sarcastically. He switched off the flashlight and shoved it into his pocket. They no longer needed it.

Besides, it couldn't really penetrate the wall of mist that had suddenly started rising out of the swamp.

"This is *great*," said Richie.

"This is creepy," said David.

And then the trail ended. Ahead of them lay a big, dark pool, half filled with green algae and viscous goo.

They stopped.

"Shh," said Richie. "Did you hear that?"

"Hear what?"

"That."

"What?" said David.

"That." Richie pointed across the pond. At the same moment, the whole earth shook, as if giant bulldozers were headed toward them.

Trex was back.

CHAPTER
10

David said, "Trex?"

"Trex!" shouted Richie happily. He started forward. David grabbed his lunatic little brother by the back of his jacket and yanked him sideways into the reeds.

"Are you crazy?" he whispered.

Trex turned his massive head. He tilted it slightly, as if he was trying to identify the sound he'd just heard. Then he straightened to his full height.

Up. Up. Up. Taller than the trees. Taller than any building in Grove Hill.

"Get *down!*" David ordered. He flattened himself among the swamp grass, pulling his brother down beside him.

Trex turned his head. His nostrils widened as if he was sniffing the air. Then he opened his mouth.

David flinched, expecting to hear a monstrous roar. But Trex didn't roar.

"He's yawning!" said Richie delightedly.

"Cute," said David, eyeing the set of choppers on the huge, meat-eating dinosaur. They made the sharks he'd seen in videos look friendly.

He was sweating. He was being eaten alive by swamp insects. He was afraid.

Scared out of his mind.

"We've got to get out of here," he said.

"Why?" said Richie. "We just found him."

"That's all we wanted to do. Find him. Now we go home and figure out what to do."

"But—"

"Listen, you, you Cretaceous Brain. We've got to go home. Go to school. Act normal. Because otherwise, people are gonna get suspicious. And if they get suspicious, they're gonna find your dinosaur. And then what do you think they're going to do?"

That stopped Richie. David watched his little brother thinking hard. At last Richie nodded. Slowly.

"Okay," he said.

"Good," said David. "Now, as soon as he looks the other way, we get invisible, right?"

It was easier said than done. Trex surveyed the scene for a long time, his big, reptilian eyes peering everywhere, his nostrils flaring. Every once in a while, the long, razor-sharp claws on his front feet would twitch. David wasn't sure, but he thought the claws looked as if they'd been used recently—like to carve up dinner.

The sun got higher in the sky.

Great, thought David. *What are the choices? Get eaten by a dinosaur or be late for school.*

Then, slowly, Trex lowered himself to the ground, balancing on his two stumpy front legs. Soon he was stretched out full-length on the ground. His head sank down. His eyelids drooped.

He yawned again. Then his mouth dropped open. A sound like a chain saw emerged from it.

Trex was snoring.

David jumped to his feet.

He crashed back down again as Richie yanked his ankle.

"It's a trick," Richie said. "Look, his eyes are open!"

David froze. It was true. Trex's huge yet beady dinosaur eyes were slitted slightly open. They gleamed watchfully from beneath the scaly lids.

And they were looking directly at David and Richie.

"I don't like this," said David. "Richie? Richie?"

Richie said, "Shhh."

Slowly, slowly, David turned his head, trying to keep his eye on Trex. Would it slow Trex down to have to wade through the swampy pool? Or could he leap the pool in a single bound?

With a huge, horrifying roar, Trex sprang to his feet and answered the question.

He could leap the pool.

"Aaaaaahhhhhhhhh!" screamed David. He rolled sideways, over and over, pulling his brother with him. The two boys flailed around in the swamp grass. At

any moment David expected to feel the sharp teeth sink into his body. He expected to be booted into the air like a soccer ball, tossed up and caught like a snack, the way Jaws Bennett ate candy.

The earth thundered as if an earthquake were happening. Trees toppled like toys. Debris rained down on them.

"Look out!" Richie hollered. He shoved David forward and into the swamp and dove in after him.

The thick, disgusting swamp goo closed over David's head. He swallowed a mouthful of something disgusting. Choking, he fought his way to the surface.

Richie was treading water beside him, his face and hair slimy with swamp water.

A roar filled the world. It hurt David's ears. Then there was the sound of an impact, as if a rocket had crashed into the earth.

Trex backed up and shook his head. He roared again at the dinosaur that stood across from him.

A dinosaur whose skull was longer than David was tall, with two horns on top and another curving up just above the nose, was standing only a few yards away at the swamp's edge. Its head was lowered. It was facing Trex.

"Bad move," muttered Richie. "Most triceratops can handle a *T. rex*. I'm sure Cyril can."

"Cyril? Cyril is your triceratops? You recognize him?" asked David thickly. He reached up and tried to wipe the goo out of his mouth, but it was no use. His hand was covered in goo, too. He tried not to think about it. The last thing he needed was to have a yak attack in the middle of a dinosaur duel.

"Of course," said Richie. "I'm glad he's all right. When I saw he was missing from the dinotank, I . . ."

Cyril lowered his head. He pawed the earth with an enormous, four-toed front foot.

Trex reared up and threw back his head. He roared at the sky.

Cyril charged.

David didn't wait to see what happened. He scrambled up out of the primeval muck of the swamp and dragged Richie with him. He was headed for the nearest dinosaur-free zone he could find.

He just hoped they would make it alive.

The hole where the back doors of Graveyard School had been was now fixed with a makeshift door. David hit the new door at top speed. It was still much too early for school, but he was hoping to find Basement Bart. Or Dr. Morthouse.

Or anybody. Even weird Mr. Lucre.

"Helpppp!" he shrieked. "Helllp. Dinosaur!"

"David!" his brother shouted behind him. "David, wait!"

"*Hellllllp!*" A classroom door on his right was open. Without even realizing which room it was, David grabbed the edge of the door frame and swung around it into the room.

Mrs. Beak's room.

Mrs. Beak was sitting at her desk. When David slid through the door, her head snapped up.

"You!" she said. "What are you doing here!"

"Dinosaur!" David gasped. "Tyrannosaurus . . . carnivore—"

"It was you. And your little brother," she said, seeing Richie. "You were the ones who started everything. I suppose this is your idea of a joke?"

"No," panted Richie. He pushed past David, ran toward the window, and peered out. He turned.

David could tell by his brother's face what Richie had seen.

"Mrs. Beak," David said urgently. "You've got to listen to us!"

"I don't have to do anything you say," she said. "Furthermore, whatever Mr. Bartholomew might say, you—you juvenile delinquents are trespassing. I'm going to call the police. They're going to lock you up and throw away the key. . . ."

Still speaking, Mrs. Beak stood up and marched over to the window. She grabbed Richie and pulled him away from it. "Go sit over there," she ordered, turning her back to the window. "At once!"

"But—"

"Now!" she barked.

His eyes so enormous they took up his entire face, Richie slowly moved back toward the desk where Mrs. Beak was pointing. When his legs hit it, he sank down into the chair as if his knees had just given way.

Mrs. Beak put her hands on her hips. She was a menacing figure, framed in the light from the classroom window, dressed all in red, from her big, pointy-toed shoes to the scarf tying back her hair.

Pretty scary.

But not nearly as scary as the huge object that suddenly blocked out all the sun coming into the room.

Mrs. Beak didn't seem to notice. She was glaring at David now.

"Sit down, I told you."

"But Mrs. Beak," David said. He swallowed hard.

"You're going to be sorry when I'm through with you." She cackled.

Slowly, slowly, the head of Trex came into focus. He lowered it and peered through the classroom window.

"Sit!" Mrs. Beak screeched.

David sat.

The head swung slowly back and forth. The huge eyes rolled. They fastened on Richie.

"No," breathed David.

Mrs. Beak advanced toward Richie, waving her arms, furious words pouring out of her mouth.

The eyes shifted from Richie to Mrs. Beak.

Then suddenly, like the paw of an enormous cat, the head of the *Tyrannosaurus rex* crashed through the classroom windows. Trex roared as the glass shattered around him. The force of the roar toppled the student desks and blew Mrs. Beak's desk sideways against the classroom door.

Everything happened so quickly that David wasn't even sure what *had* happened . . . just that one minute, Mrs. Beak was shouting at Richie and him.

And the next, she was shrieking in an entirely different tone of voice.

Then her voice stopped in midshriek.

Then she disappeared. Except for one red shoe, which dropped to the floor as the dinosaur jerked his head out of the window.

"Wow," breathed Richie.

"Oh, no!" shouted David. He raced to the window. He scrambled out.

But it was too late. Mrs. Beak was gone.

CHAPTER

11

Feeling as if he were moving in super-slow motion, David ran to the window in time to see Trex stride casually across the teachers' parking lot.

He stepped on the roof of Mrs. Beak's huge, gas-guzzling car and flattened it.

Then he stopped. He threw back his head and roared his horrible roar.

Richie's voice spoke at David's elbow. "It's Cyril."

The triceratops had apparently followed the tyrannosaurus. It was standing at the top of Graveyard Hill.

Trex didn't wait. He charged eagerly up the hill in what seemed like two giant steps, kicking aside tombstones as if they were marshmallows.

David and Richie turned and ran out of the school after Trex.

As they scrambled up through the graveyard, Trex reached the top of the hill.

Cyril rushed forward and the two dinosaurs collided. More tombstones tipped over.

"Watch out!" David cried, his voice almost lost in the terrible noise. Richie skipped out of the way of a falling angel at the last minute, and the two brothers kept on going.

They'd just reached the top of the hill when a blinding flash of light stopped them.

David threw up his hands. Richie crashed into him from behind. They both fell forward.

And the world was still.

Quiet.

Peaceful even.

David wondered if the dinosaur had gotten him.

"David?" his little brother whispered. "Are you dead?"

"Nope," said David. He was surprised to realize it was true. Slowly he opened his eyes.

And screamed more loudly than he'd ever screamed in his whole life.

A kid who looked *exactly* like him was standing there.

The kid tilted his head. "Why are you screaming?" he asked David in David's voice.

"*Aaaaaah!*" David answered. "*Aaaaarrrrgh!*"

"Where's Trex? Where's Cyril? What have you done with my dinosaurs?" Richie demanded shrilly. Then he, too, stopped. He didn't scream.

He just watched silently as a kid who looked exactly

like him, right down to the drying swamp goo stuck to his clothes, came to stand face-to-face with him.

The two sets of twins stood there for a long moment. Then David swallowed and looked around.

"Who are you?"

"It is not important. This is just a form we choose because we thought it would be less threatening to you."

"Where are my dinosaurs? What did you do with my dinosaurs?" Richie said. One thing about Richie, David thought. He never gave up.

Richie's twin answered, "There." He pointed.

They both looked.

A large, sponge-shaped object was hovering inches above Landings Road.

"Odd," said Richie's twin. "This was an island in a huge swamp when we left. We weren't gone that long."

David's twin shook his head. "True. But time is different at different coordinates."

"Huh?" said David. It was all he could manage.

His twin went on speaking. "A huge, swampy, marshy plain. We wanted two of everything, you see. At least two. The future of the planet did not look good."

He stopped and looked down at Graveyard School. His eyes narrowed. "Hmmm." Then he said, almost to himself, "Perhaps the exercise of collecting a specimen of current negative-impact low life-form for study was not such a bad idea."

99

Richie's twin said, "But when we had traveled only a few years, we discovered that not only had we left behind two, but also one of our own.

"Fortunately, he was able to survive and to preserve the two, as well as a number of others in a primitive suspended compressed form. The form could be reestablished only by the approach of the light-particle beam we use in low-field navigation."

David's twin took up the story. "Unfortunately, upon our arrival, we discovered that a human assistant of his had stolen some of our animals and tried to make some money off them by selling them in a mail-order business . . . a most annoying business.

"We were forced to seek out and collect them. In most cases, it was merely a time-consuming annoyance. But in yours, I am afraid, our approach triggered the decompression process."

"Where are my dino—"

"In the Transpod, of course," said Richie's twin. "They've been happily reunited with their families and fellows of their species. Soon they will be part of a new planet in a new galaxy. One that is more hospitable to intelligent life, naturally."

"Naturally," David managed to say. Then he said, "Trex, uh, ate, uh . . . I think the tyrannosaurus ate a teacher."

"Oh, no," said Richie's twin. "No, no, no. What happened was we—uh!"

His partner had elbowed him in the side. Smoothly the partner took over. "We thank you for the very good care you took, our friends. We have gathered all the missing, I trust." He paused and gave Richie's twin a sharp look. And Richie's twin nodded quickly, just as Richie did when he didn't want to get in trouble. *To avoid trouble,* David thought, *Richie would agree to anything.*

But David's twin, who was apparently in charge, did not seem to notice. He turned back to David and Richie. "Perhaps we will meet again."

The two turned and strode toward the Transpod.

"Wait!" cried Richie. "Wait. Does this mean that Trex and Cyril really are real? That the dinosaurs *aren't* extinct?"

Looking back, Richie's twin nodded. Then he grinned a big, friendly alien grin. "Of course not!" he said. He stared into Richie's eyes and then quickly winked. "And don't worry. They'll be back."

There was another blinding flash of light. Then the two creatures and their Transpod were gone.

David and Richie stood there in stunned silence.

Suddenly a movement caught the corner of David's eye. He turned. Down below, a car door slammed. Dr. Morthouse got out and put her hands on her hips, surveying the new damage to her school.

"C'mon," David said. "We've got to get out of here!"

• • •

"Two days with no school," Raul said jubilantly. "Did you hear what they said on the news? They think an *earthquake* hit the school. Like major."

He stopped. He looked at David and Richie suspiciously.

". . . an earthquake," said David. "Want some more soda?"

The three of them were eating lunch at the Pikes' house. Afterward they were going to hang out at the park.

Richie yawned.

Raul said, "They think the earthquake might have gotten Mrs. Beak. No one's seen her. She just disappeared without a trace. Except for her shoe. Isn't that weird? They found one of her shoes in the classroom. That's it."

"Did they recycle it?" David asked.

Raul laughed so hard that he almost choked and David had to pound him on the back. "Good one, good one," Raul said.

Relieved at having diverted Raul, David quickly finished his lunch and stood up. "Let's go," he said.

Richie shook his head slowly. "I'm gonna go upstairs to my room and do some research," he said.

"Suit yourself," said David. He gave Richie a warning look. Richie made a face back. They'd been over it and over it, and Richie knew he had to keep quiet.

No one would have believed them anyway.

Would they have?

David and Raul left. Richie yawned. He was tired.

He went slowly up the stairs. At the door of his room, he stopped and stared at the empty space where the dinotank had been. It would be a long, long time before he'd ever be able to replace it.

All that was left was the box that his dinosaurs—his *real* dinosaurs—had come in, sitting forlornly on the chest where the dinotank had been.

Oh well. At least Trex and Cyril were back with their families. At least they were going to a good home.

Richie picked up the box and sat in the chair by the window with the box in his arms. He sighed. He looked down into it. His eyes widened.

Then he began to smile.

There, in the bottom of the box, was a tiny, perfect dinosaur.

Can you unscramble these dinosaur names?

Hint: They're all mentioned in *Revenge of the Dinosaurs!*

1. SOURLAMASAU
2. STOPATCIRRE
3. YOURREARSUNNS TAX
4. PARTAUSASOA